THE PUPPY PLACE

BELLA

THE PUPPY PLACE

Baxter
Bear
Bella
Buddy
Chewy and Chica
Cody
Flash
Goldie
Honey
Jack
Lucky
Maggie and Max
Muttley
Noodle
Patches
Princess
Pugsley
Rascal
Scout
Shadow
Snowball
Sweetie
Ziggy

THE PUPPY PLACE

BELLA

ELLEN MILES

SCHOLASTIC INC.
New York   Toronto   London   Auckland
Sydney   Mexico City   New Delhi   Hong Kong

For Kailyn and Maxx

ISBN 978-0-545-25396-3

Cover art by Tim O'Brien
Original cover design by Steve Scott

12 11 10 9 8 7 6   11 12 13 14 15 16/0

Printed in the U.S.A.   40

First printing, February 2011

CHAPTER ONE

"Happy birthday, dear Maria," sang Lizzie, along with everyone else. "Happy birthday to you!"

Lizzie gave Maria a special smile as she sang. There were a lot of kids at the party—almost everybody in their class was there—but everyone knew that Lizzie Peterson and Maria Santiago were best friends. They sat next to each other in class, played on the same kickball team at recess, and always ate lunch together. They had the same favorite color (purple) and the same lucky number (eight). They both loved fudge ripple ice cream, cool socks, snowstorms, and reading.

Most of all, Lizzie and Maria loved animals. That was why Maria had decided to have her birthday party at Caring Paws, the animal shelter where she and Lizzie both volunteered. It was Lizzie's idea: she had gotten all excited when she had read about a boy who had his party at a shelter. "Instead of presents," she'd told Maria, "everybody brought donations for the animals."

Maria wasn't so sure at first. "Why don't you do it for *your* birthday?" she'd asked Lizzie.

"I will, but mine's not for months and yours is coming right up. I know your real birthday isn't until Monday, but we can have the party on Saturday. Come on, it'll be fun! We can play animal-themed games, and decorate the meeting room with colorful paw prints, and have a dog bone–shaped cake, and everything." Lizzie was full of ideas, and she could be very convincing. "It's a great Caring Club activity, too. Think of all the donations you'll get for the shelter.

Ms. Dobbins will be very happy." Ms. Dobbins was the shelter's director.

When Lizzie had started the Caring Club, Maria had been one of the first to join. Caring Club was for kids who loved animals and wanted to help them.

Maria's favorite animals were horses. She loved to ride, and she spent a lot of time at the stable. Lizzie had gone with her a few times, and had even taken riding lessons for a while, but she had never learned to love horses as much as she loved dogs.

Lizzie really, really loved dogs.

In fact, Lizzie was dog-crazy.

She collected model dogs. She had a whole shelf of books about dogs and dog training. She had a "Dog Breeds of the World" poster hanging over her bed. And, best of all, she had a dog of her very own: Buddy, the cutest puppy in the history of the universe. Buddy was a sweet, gentle, funny, medium-sized mutt, mostly brown but with a heart-shaped white patch on his chest. Lizzie adored him, and so did the rest of the family: her mom, her dad, and her younger brothers, Charles and the Bean (whose actual name was Adam).

The Petersons had first met Buddy when he came to them as a foster puppy along with his two sisters and their dog mom. The Petersons had fostered lots of puppies; that meant they took care of puppies who needed homes, just until they found each puppy the perfect forever family. But they had all fallen in love with Buddy, so they had decided to keep him.

Maria had a dog, too—or rather, her mother did. Simba, a big yellow Lab, was a Seeing Eye dog. He was trained to help Mrs. Santiago, who was blind. With Simba, Mrs. Santiago could cross busy streets, do grocery shopping, go for a hike in the woods—anything! Simba wasn't exactly a pet, but he was a smart, good dog. He was there now at Maria's birthday party, helping guide Mrs. Santiago as she carried a bone-shaped chocolate cake to the table while everyone sang.

Maria shut her eyes, made a wish (Lizzie knew it was for a horse of her own), and blew out the candles. She had just started to cut the first slice when Ms. Dobbins opened the door and poked her head into the room. "I can tell you're having a good time in here," she said, smiling. "I wanted to thank you all for the donations. The animals and I appreciate your generosity." She waved a hand at the pile of donations that the party guests had brought. It took up a whole corner of the room.

Lizzie looked at the pile and beamed. Right out in front she saw the fifty-pound bag of dog food she and her mom had lugged in, and a cat carrier that Brianna had brought. Daphne had contributed some brand-new dog toys, and Noah had saved up his allowance to buy ten leashes and collars.

Jimmy and Daniel had chipped in for a new cat tower, and Shanna and her dad had brought five cases of canned cat food.

"And I especially thank Maria, for having her birthday here," Ms. Dobbins finished. "Most kids would rather have presents for themselves, but this shows that you really do care about animals."

Maria smiled. "I like presents, too," she said. "But I'll get some from my family."

Lizzie happened to know that Maria would also be getting a very cool pair of purple and green striped socks. She'd bought them yesterday, along with a matching pair for herself, and planned to give them to Maria on Monday, her real birthday.

"Ms. Dobbins! Ms. Dobbins!" Someone yelled from the front desk. "She's here!"

"Oops, better go!" said Ms. Dobbins. "We've got a bit of an emergency on our hands. But have a great time—and save me a piece of cake!"

Lizzie wondered what was going on. What kind of emergency was it? Was one of the animals sick? "She's here!" could mean that the vet, Dr. Gibson, had arrived. Or maybe it was Jan the plumber, if the dog-washing sink was stopped up again. Or had a cat escaped from the cat room and been caught near the front desk? Should she go help?

No, Ms. Dobbins seemed to be on top of things. Lizzie turned her attention back to the party. Once the singing and cake part was over, it would be time for games. Lizzie couldn't wait for the animal-themed treasure hunt she and Maria had planned.

When the party was over, and Maria's father had picked her and her mom up to take them to her grandparents' house for a birthday dinner, Lizzie finally had the chance to ask Ms. Dobbins about the emergency. "What happened?" she asked.

"We had a very special new arrival," said Ms. Dobbins. She put her finger over her lips as she cracked open the door to her office so Lizzie could peek inside. "Shhh! She's asleep."

At first Lizzie didn't know what Ms. Dobbins was talking about. Then she gasped. "Oh! She's so little," she whispered. Under Ms. Dobbins's desk, a tiny puppy lay sleeping, tucked inside a shoebox lined with an old towel.

CHAPTER TWO

They slipped quietly into the office, and Lizzie knelt down to take a closer look at the puppy in the shoebox. Ms. Dobbins had set up a lamp over the box to keep her warm. In the lamp's golden glow, the puppy stretched and squirmed in her sleep. She opened her tiny mouth and yawned a pink puppy yawn. Lizzie felt her heart flip over. The puppy was only a few inches long, and mostly white with orangey-red spots like freckles. One ear was the same orangey-red color and the other was white. Her nose was pink, and her tiny paws were, too. Her ears were just little flaps, about the size of Lizzie's pinky fingernail.

Now the puppy opened her mouth and made a little mewing noise, almost like a kitten. "Oh!" said Lizzie. The puppy looked up at her with milky blue eyes that did not quite seem to focus on her face. "Wow, her eyes are barely open." She wanted to reach out a finger and stroke the puppy, but she was afraid she might hurt her. "How old is she?"

"Just under four weeks," said Ms. Dobbins.

"Where's her mom?" Lizzie knew that a puppy that age needs to be with her mother. She needs her milk, and she needs her warmth and her care. "Doesn't she have any sisters and brothers?"

Ms. Dobbins sighed. "Her mother is very sick," she said. "That's why she's here." She sat down on the floor next to Lizzie. "Right before Maria's party started, I got a call from my old friend Alexandra, who lives about two hours away. Her cocker spaniel Sissy had puppies, but Sissy got sick right before she gave birth, and she is still sick, too sick to take care of them properly." She paused and gave Lizzie a very serious look. "Sissy had five puppies, this one here plus four boys. But none of the boys made it."

"You mean—they died?" Lizzie asked. She could hardly stand to think about it. Poor puppies! Poor little girl, all alone in the world without her mom or her brothers.

Ms. Dobbins nodded. "It's so sad. Alexandra kept hoping that Sissy would get better, and she is improving. But Sissy still can't take care of this last puppy, and neither can Alexandra. She's too busy taking care of Sissy."

Lizzie looked down at the puppy. She didn't look much at all like the cocker spaniels on her "Dog Breeds of the World" poster, with their long, fringed ears and adorable faces. She looked more

11

like a hamster. A sick hamster. "The poor little thing!"

"I know," said Ms. Dobbins. "When Alexandra called to ask for help, I agreed to take her. How could I say no? Her friend drove the puppy up and showed me how to mix the formula to feed her with." She showed Lizzie a baby bottle full of white liquid. "It's made with goat's milk and raw eggs," she said. "And some other stuff. Puppies this age have to eat every three or four hours. Maybe even more often in this case, since she is not growing as fast as she should be."

"She does seem really small," said Lizzie. She gazed down at the puppy, feeling a strange mixture of love and fear. This small, squirmy thing was so helpless!

Ms. Dobbins nodded. "She's had a tough life so far and she's not very strong."

"What's her name?" Lizzie asked.

"She doesn't have a name yet. Alexandra wanted to wait to see how she does." Ms. Dobbins put out one finger to pet the tiny puppy.

"How she does?" asked Lizzie. She felt an ache in the back of her throat. "You mean—"

Ms. Dobbins nodded. "I have to warn you, Lizzie. This puppy might not make it. Normally a four-week puppy can survive without her dog mom, as long as she has plenty of care from a human. But since Sissy was sick ever since she was born, this pup has not had a very easy start in life."

Lizzie swallowed. The ache in her throat was worse now, and her eyes felt hot. "But you'll take good care of her," she said. "Right?"

"I'll do my best," said Ms. Dobbins. She stood up and dusted off her hands. "I think it's time to get her settled at home. The staff can close up here today. I'll grab all the formula supplies if you can carry the box out to my car."

"Me?" Lizzie asked. Lizzie knew so much about dog breeds, and dog training, and dog care. But somehow, this tiny puppy made her feel as if she did not know anything at all. She was not sure she trusted herself to carry that box without dropping it or jarring the puppy inside.

Ms. Dobbins smiled. "Yes, you," she said. "You'll be fine." She arranged another towel over the top of the box to keep the puppy warm, then picked the box up and handed it to Lizzie. "Follow me," she said.

Lizzie followed Ms. Dobbins, cradling the box carefully in her arms. It wasn't heavy at all; it probably weighed less than her math book. Lizzie felt the box move a little as the puppy squirmed around inside. Out in the parking lot, she followed Ms. Dobbins's directions and gently set the box on the floor by the passenger seat.

"Okay, Lizzie. Thanks. I'll let you know how she's doing."

Lizzie watched as Ms. Dobbins drove off. When her mom pulled in a few seconds later to pick her up, Lizzie burst into tears.

Her mom jumped out of the car. "What is it, honey?" She hugged Lizzie close. "Did something go wrong at the party?"

Lizzie cried even harder, burying her face into her mother's familiar soft warmth. When she could speak, she told Mom about the puppy.

"Oh, sweetie," said Mom. "That's so hard." She hugged Lizzie some more. "Tell you what. I could use your help in the kitchen this afternoon. Let's go to the store, and then we'll get busy. It'll help keep your mind off the puppy."

Lizzie followed Mom around the store, then helped her unpack the groceries at home and set out all the things they needed to make lasagna.

"I'm making two," Mom explained. "One for us and one for our new neighbors. I saw the moving van arrive earlier today, and now there's a car in the driveway. I'm sure a nice, easy dinner would be a welcome gift."

Ordinarily, Lizzie would have been curious about who had moved into the house next door, which was so close that she could almost reach out and touch it from the kitchen window. But today it didn't seem important.

"Okay," she said. She knew Mom was trying to distract her, but it was not working too well. She stirred tomato sauce, and shredded cheese, and laid out lasagna noodles, but the whole time she was thinking about the puppy at Ms. Dobbins's house. What was she doing now? Was she eating well from the bottle? Was she warm enough? Lizzie almost burst out crying again, thinking how much the puppy must be missing her mom and brothers.

When the lasagna was done, Mom wrapped it in foil and put a note on top. *Cook at 350 for one hour, until cheese is bubbly. Welcome to the neighborhood!* Then she asked Lizzie to deliver the lasagna while she cleaned up the kitchen.

Lizzie carried the heavy pan across the neighbors' yard and knocked at the front door. Nobody answered. She waited for a few moments and knocked again. No footsteps came down the stairs. The house seemed completely silent. She wasn't sure what to do, but finally she decided to set the lasagna on a small bench on the porch. Hopefully someone would come home soon and see it.

When she came back to the house, Mom was standing in the kitchen, looking upset.

"What is it?" Lizzie's heart thumped wildly. "Mom! What happened? Did the puppy die?"

Mom shook her head, and Lizzie felt a wave of relief.

"But she's not doing well. Ms. Dobbins just called," Mom said. "The puppy is having a hard time learning to drink from the bottle. Ms. Dobbins called the vet, but she wanted to be sure you knew ahead of time that the puppy really might not make it."

CHAPTER THREE

Lizzie swallowed hard. The poor little puppy. First she lost her brothers, then her mother was too sick to take care of her, and now she might— Lizzie couldn't even bear to think about it. It just wasn't fair. It wasn't fair at all.

"I'm sorry, honey," Mom said, stroking her back. "But maybe she'll be okay. Let's try to be hopeful."

"Ms. Dobbins must be really worried." said Lizzie.

Mom nodded. "She is. I know you probably want to talk to her, but let's wait until morning. She has her hands full trying to keep that puppy alive."

Charles and the Bean were upset when they heard, too—even though they had never even seen the puppy. And Lizzie could tell that her dad felt terrible. At dinner, while everybody picked at the lasagna (they all seemed to have lost their appetites), he talked about the first pet he'd ever had, a turtle named Finkle. "I loved Finkle so much," he said. "I would spend hours holding her in my hand, feeding her lettuce and petting her little shell."

Lizzie wasn't into turtles, but she could tell that Dad had really cared for this one. "What happened?" she asked.

"One morning, when I went to get Finkle out of her tank, she wasn't moving. I didn't know why at first, and my dad had to explain that Finkle was never going to move again. First I didn't believe it. Then I was sad." Dad looked sad now, remembering.

Lizzie went over to give him a hug. "I'm sorry, Daddy," she said. Charles and the Bean jumped up to hug him, too, and Buddy sat up and put a paw on Dad's lap. Soon Dad was smiling again.

That night, Lizzie did not sleep well at all. She tossed and turned, wondering if the girl puppy was going to make it. When she woke up, the sun was streaming through her windows. It was late!

Lizzie pulled a sweatshirt on over her pajamas and ran downstairs. "Can we call Ms. Dobbins?" she asked Mom, before she even said good morning.

"I've already spoken to her." Mom put down the newspaper she was reading.

Lizzie squeezed her eyes shut, held her breath, and crossed her fingers tight.

"The puppy made it through the night," Mom said.

Lizzie opened her eyes and let out a big whoosh of breath.

Mom smiled at her. "In fact, she's doing great. Once Dr. Gibson helped Ms. Dobbins get the puppy used to the bottle feeding, she ate and ate—every two hours!" Mom pushed back her chair and got up to pour herself more coffee. "Dr. Gibson said it's not unusual for puppies to get stronger very quickly once they start eating well," she said.

"Oh, Mom. She made it!" Lizzie threw her arms around her mother.

"You were really worried about her, weren't you?" Mom said.

Lizzie nodded. "Can we go see her today?" she asked.

"Well," said Mom, "that's the next piece of news. When Ms. Dobbins called, she told me that she has realized that she just can't take care of a newborn puppy and also do her job.

She was up practically all night, and she is exhausted."

"But what will happen to the puppy?" Lizzie pushed away from her mom and stared up at her.

Mom put her hands on Lizzie's shoulders. She smiled. "We're going to take her," she said.

Lizzie stared at her mother, speechless.

"We can split up the work. It's too much for one person, but if Dad and I and you and Charles all help out, I think we can manage." Mom raised her eyebrows. "What do you think?"

"I think—I think it's great!" Lizzie finally managed to get some words out. She was so surprised that Mom had agreed to take the puppy. This would really be something new, to foster such a young puppy. Lizzie was excited—and scared. Fostering other puppies had sometimes been a little bit challenging, but mostly it had been great fun. This was different. Taking care of a newborn seemed like such a big responsibility.

What if the girl puppy died, the way her brothers had?

But when Ms. Dobbins came over with the puppy, Lizzie was too busy to be scared. There was so much to learn! How to mix up the formula, and heat it to the perfect temperature. How to poke the right-size holes in the baby bottle's nipple. How to keep the puppy's box clean by changing the newspaper, and how to keep the puppy clean by wiping her with a soft, damp cloth. How to set up a lamp and a hot water bottle to keep the puppy warm—but not *too* warm. And how to mix up a mess of soaked puppy chow and water. Ms. Dobbins called it "slurry," and Lizzie and Mom would have to start feeding it to the puppy. Each day she would get a little more slurry and a little less formula. That was called "weaning," and with luck the puppy would not need the bottle much longer. Ms. Dobbins talked Mom and Lizzie through it all. (Dad had taken Charles and Buddy and the Bean out for the day, so the puppy's home-coming would be quieter.)

The girl puppy did look much, much better. Her belly was round and full and she actually seemed to have grown in the hours since Lizzie had last seen her. She cried a lot—probably because she missed her mom and her brothers—but she also moved around more, staggering uncertainly on her little legs, with her tiny, pointed tail sticking straight up in the air.

"Go ahead and pick her up," Ms. Dobbins urged Lizzie. "It's good for her to be handled now."

"Really?" Lizzie had never felt nervous about holding a puppy before. Carefully, gently, she picked the puppy up and held her close to her chest. Lizzie could feel the puppy's heart beating fast. "It's okay, little one," she murmured. "It's okay." She felt her own heart fill with love for this tiny thing, all alone in the world. The puppy snuggled against her.

I feel so safe with you.

"You know," said Ms. Dobbins, smiling down at Lizzie and the puppy. "I think this puppy needs a name."

Lizzie looked up. "Really? Are you sure?" That must mean that Ms. Dobbins thought that the puppy would not die.

Ms. Dobbins nodded. "Dr. Gibson said that if she made it through last night, it's a pretty good bet that she'll do just fine from here on out, especially with your loving care."

The puppy nuzzled her head into Lizzie's chest, let out a tiny sigh, and fell asleep.

"Good girl, Bella," said Lizzie.

Bella. The perfect name for a beautiful little girl.

CHAPTER FOUR

Ms. Dobbins stayed long enough to supervise while Lizzie fed Bella for the first time. Then she had to go. "You're doing great," she told Lizzie. "Bella is really going to thrive, now that she's met you."

By then, Lizzie knew that "thrive" meant to gain weight and grow strong. To live. She gazed down at the puppy, who lay on a thick, folded towel in her lap. Bella's tummy was round and full of formula, and she slept soundly, curled into a warm, soft ball. "Bella," she whispered, and the puppy's tiny ears twitched. Lizzie felt her heart swell again. This little creature needed her so badly.

When Ms. Dobbins left, Mom went upstairs to

work on an article. Lizzie sat on the couch with Bella on her lap, watching the puppy's chest rise and fall with every small breath she took. Sometimes there was a pause between breaths, and Lizzie's heart would begin to pound. What would she do if Bella stopped breathing? But then Bella would wriggle a bit and give a little puppy snort and her breaths would come regularly again.

After a while, Lizzie's foot fell asleep. When she shifted her position, Bella woke up—and immediately began to cry. She clawed her way up Lizzie's shirt, mewing like a kitten and weaving her little head back and forth as if she were looking for something.

Feed me, feed me!

She *was* looking for something, Lizzie realized. Something to eat! "Mom!" Lizzie called. "Bella's hungry."

Mom came downstairs to help Lizzie warm the formula and fill a bottle. When Lizzie put the nipple near Bella's mouth, she latched on right away and did not stop sucking until the bottle was empty. When she was done, she yawned and began to curl up on Lizzie's lap again. But Lizzie tucked her into her cozy box and set up the lamp over her to keep her warm. "You sleep for a little while," she told Bella, "while I take care of some other things."

Lizzie needed to wrap the socks she'd gotten for Maria. Also, Mom had been bugging her to clean her room, and it really did need it. Lizzie had to admit that things had gotten a little out of control in there lately. She knew she had some homework to do, but at the moment she wasn't even sure where her backpack was. Cleanup would have to come first.

But Bella did not seem happy in her box. As soon as Lizzie took one step away, she woke up and began to cry. Lizzie came back and stroked Bella's head with one finger until the puppy calmed down. Lizzie still could not believe how tiny Bella was. Her head was hardly bigger than a golf ball. When Bella's eyes fell shut and her breaths got longer, Lizzie took her finger away and stood up again. The puppy's eyes popped open, her pink mouth yawned wide, and she began to whimper and whine. She struggled to her feet and tried to scrabble her way out of the box, crying in the most pitiful, pathetic way.

Lonely! I'm so lonely. Pleeeease don't leave me here alone.

"Oh, Bella." Lizzie sighed and picked the puppy up out of her box. She cradled her close as she walked back to the couch. Bella's cries stopped as soon as Lizzie held her, but the puppy's heart pumped hard and fast; it felt like hummingbird wings against Lizzie's chest.

Lizzie sat down, trying to settle herself more comfortably this time, now that she knew Bella was not about to let her move or go away. For the rest of the afternoon Lizzie held the puppy as Bella slept and woke, cried and ate, cried some more, slept some more, and ate some more.

"You look exhausted," Mom said when she came downstairs again to check on Lizzie and Bella.

"She won't let me leave her, even for a minute." Lizzie felt that now-familiar ache in her throat, and her eyes filled with tears. "And I'm afraid she's going to die if I'm not with her all the time. She's so little. It feels like anything could happen."

Mom nodded. "I know exactly how you feel." She sat down next to Lizzie on the couch. "Know why? Because that's how I felt when I brought

31

you home from the hospital the day after you were born."

Lizzie stared at her mom. "Really?"

Mom smiled and pushed the hair back from Lizzie's face. "Really. Your dad was much more confident, but I was a mess. I felt totally overwhelmed by the responsibility. I mean, here I was, practically alone with this tiny creature who would not survive without my care!"

Lizzie leaned against her mom. "But I did survive."

"And it looks like Bella will, too," Mom said. "Remember, you're not alone in this. Dad and I will take care of her through the night so you can get your sleep. And I know Charles wants to help, too."

"I already figured out his job," Lizzie said. "When he and Dad get home, Charles can help keep Buddy and the Bean away from Bella.

Ms. Dobbins said we should keep them apart, and I'm afraid they might hurt her by mistake."

"Good thinking," Mom said. "Now, do you want me to hold her for a while?"

Lizzie shook her head. "That's okay." As tired as she was, Lizzie felt bonded to Bella in a way that was different from the bond she'd had with any other foster puppy. As long as she was awake, she wanted to be with Bella.

CHAPTER FIVE

At her desk the next day, Lizzie could not stop yawning.

"You look exhausted," Maria whispered from her seat next to Lizzie's.

Lizzie gave her friend a weak smile. It had been nearly twenty-four hours since Mom had said exactly the same thing to her, and Lizzie felt as if she'd been awake every one of those hours. She *was* exhausted. Taking care of Bella was wearing her out. Mom and Dad were supposedly covering the night shifts with the puppy, but Lizzie could not help waking up every time she heard Bella cry. She had ended up helping out with feedings many times through the night.

Lizzie had not told Maria about Bella. What if the puppy died? Maria did not need to hear such a sad thing on her birthday. It wasn't easy to keep this big secret from her best friend, but it felt like the right thing to do.

Now Mrs. Abeson stood up at the front of the classroom. "Time!" she called out. "You can put your notebooks away and get ready for recess. We'll work some more on our Persuasive Essays tomorrow."

Lizzie put down her pen with a sigh. She was supposed to be writing a one-page paper that would convince people to agree with her point of view. When the essays were done, they were all going to have to read them aloud. The topic she'd chosen was "Why Dogs Make the Best Friends." She had a long list of very good reasons, but truthfully the essay was boring. Who needed to be convinced about how great dogs were, anyway? Everybody knew that. Lizzie yawned again. Maybe she would have to try another topic.

"Kiddos who want to go outside, may," said Mrs. Abeson, glancing out the window at the gray, drizzly sky. "But if you'd rather stay in the classroom for recess today, that's fine, too."

Lizzie definitely wanted to stay inside. She did not have the energy today for a wet, muddy game of kickball. Anyway, she wanted to give Maria her present. She reached into her desk and pulled out the socks, which were still in the store bag. "Happy birthday," she said, handing them to Maria. "Sorry they're not wrapped. I've been kind of busy."

Maria grinned when she opened the bag and pulled out the socks. "These are so cool," she said. "Thanks!" Then she put them down. "So, what's going on?"

Lizzie was ready for the question. Even though she was keeping a secret from her best friend, she did have something to tell. Something very interesting. "There's a mystery next door," she said. "Something strange is going on."

"Really?" Maria looked interested. "What?"

"I—um—happened to wake up at four-thirty this morning. And I saw lights on at our neighbor's house. You know, the Schneiders', next door? They moved out last month, and somebody new just moved in. I could see a person moving around downstairs in the kitchen: taking food out of the oven, setting the table, sitting down to eat. A little while after that, the shades went down and all the lights went out, first downstairs and then upstairs."

"Huh," said Maria. "It's like they're doing everything backwards, having dinner in the morning and then going to bed."

"Exactly," said Lizzie. "But why?"

Maria looked even more interested. "I wish it were a weekend so I could sleep over. We could stay up all night and spy."

Lizzie and Maria had recently read *Harriet the Spy*, and they were thinking of going into the spy business themselves. Lizzie had bought a note-book for taking things down (it had a collie on the cover) and Maria had asked for a flashlight for her birthday.

"Mm-hmm," said Lizzie. It was just as well that Maria couldn't sleep over, since then the secret about Bella would be out. "Too bad. But I'll keep an eye out myself and let you know what happens."

Lizzie's heart fluttered as she pushed open the door when she got home from school that day. Had Bella made it through the day? The house was very quiet. Where was the puppy? Buddy came running into the hallway to greet her, but before she could even ruffle his ears and say hello, he dashed back toward the living room. "Mom?" Lizzie called.

"In here." Mom was in the living room, with Bella in her lap. She looked very tired. Buddy padded around the room, unable to sit still. He whimpered a little and put a paw up on the couch, trying to get close to Bella. "No, Buddy." Mom sighed. "It's been a long day," she told Lizzie. "Bella cried almost constantly, and it's been like a full-time job to keep Buddy away from her. Your dad is napping now so he can do the first night shift."

"But Bella looks good." Lizzie picked up the tiny pup. "Check it out! I think she has three new freckles." Ms. Dobbins had explained that as she grew, Bella's coat would show more and more red spots. Lizzie kissed Bella's round, soft tummy. "I can tell that she ate well today, too." Lizzie thought Bella might have gained at least a pound since she had first seen her.

"She did," said Mom. "I really think she's going to make it."

"I do, too," said Lizzie. But she sounded more certain than she felt. Bella was still the youngest puppy the Petersons had ever fostered, and she needed so much care. Lizzie was tired, and so were Mom and Dad. How long could they give Bella the attention she needed?

A little bit later, Lizzie held Bella while Mom mixed up some puppy chow slurry. Charles had gotten home by then and he was trying hard to keep Buddy away from Bella, distracting him with toys and treats. But it was like Buddy was magnetically attached to the newborn pup. When the food was ready, Lizzie brought Bella into the kitchen to eat. Buddy followed close at her heels. "Charles!" Lizzie yelled. "Come get Buddy!"

Bella ate, slurping greedily. "She likes it," Lizzie said.

"Good," Mom said. "The more of this she eats, the fewer bottles we'll have to give her."

"And the better she'll sleep." Lizzie held up both hands, fingers crossed. "Hopefully."

But Bella's cries woke Lizzie over and over again in the night. No matter how full her tummy was, Bella seemed to need to be held whenever she woke up. Mom and Dad kept telling Lizzie to stay in bed, but how could she sleep when she knew Bella needed her?

Finally, at five in the morning, Lizzie decided she might as well stay up for good. She carried Bella's box downstairs. While she was in the kitchen mixing up slurry, she saw the front door open at the new neighbor's house, where all the lights were already on. A girl with long, black hair stepped out onto the porch. Lizzie's eyebrows went up. Had a girl her age moved in next door? A girl who stayed up all night and slept all day? The mystery was growing.

For a second, Lizzie thought about running upstairs to get her spy notebook, but she realized she was too tired to take notes. Instead, she decided to take the easy way out. Picking up

Bella, she went to her own front door and slipped outside.

The girl on the porch next door must have spotted Lizzie. She waved, then held up one finger in the "wait-a-minute" sign. Then she disappeared inside.

CHAPTER SIX

When she came back out, the girl was holding Mom's lasagna pan. She carried it across the driveway in her robe and pajamas and slippers. As she got closer, Lizzie realized that she wasn't a girl at all. She was a woman, an Asian woman with a very small build and long black hair. Lizzie was disappointed. She had begun to think she might have a new friend next door.

The woman smiled shyly as she handed over the clean, empty pan. "That was the best lasagna I ever had," she said. "I ate a ton of it and there was still some left over to freeze for another meal. Please thank your mother. Did you help make it?"

Lizzie nodded. "It's Mom's recipe. But I've helped her lots of times. I could probably even make it myself."

"I'm Tina Wu," said the woman, sticking out her hand.

"I'm Lizzie Peterson." Lizzie fumbled with Bella so she could shake hands with Tina. "And this is Bella," she added.

Tina gasped. "I didn't even see her! What a tiny puppy. She must be a newborn. Is that her mom, the cute little brown dog I've seen in your backyard?"

Lizzie giggled. "No, that's our puppy, Buddy. He's very interested in Bella, but we have to keep him away because she's so young and he could hurt her by mistake. Bella is a foster puppy. She's only four weeks old. Her mom is very sick so we're raising her by hand, feeding her from a bottle."

Tina raised her eyebrows. "That can't be easy."

44

"It's not," said Lizzie. "But I'm glad we're doing it. It's a real experience, that's for sure. We have fostered lots of puppies, but never a newborn."

Tina sat down on the Petersons' front steps. "Could I hold her for a second? I've never held a puppy that young. I don't know if I've ever *seen* a puppy that young."

Carefully, Lizzie passed Bella over. "She's very sleepy, since she just ate." Lizzie stretched out her arms and yawned.

"You look pretty sleepy yourself," Tina said to Lizzie as she cradled Bella. She bent to nuzzle the puppy's head. "Oh, her fur is so soft. She's lovely."

"She'd be lovelier if she would sleep through the night," said Lizzie. "She cries all the time. I guess she's lonely." She told Tina about how Bella's brothers had died.

"Poor girl," Tina said. "I bet she misses them a lot. I can just picture a bunch of puppies snuggling together with their mom. It wouldn't be easy for humans to make up for that kind of warmth and connection." She turned her face to the rising sun. "Here it comes," she said. "Don't you love to watch the sun come up?"

Lizzie laughed. "I don't see that happen too much. I'm usually in bed. I like sunsets, though."

"I don't see much of the sun at all," said Tina. "I work for a Chinese company, and they are twelve hours ahead of us, so I'm in my home office all night emailing back and forth. Then I have dinner at 5 A.M. or so, and go to bed soon after the sun rises." She shrugged and laughed. "It's kind of weird, I know. But I'm used to it."

The mystery was solved, just like that. Lizzie couldn't wait to tell Maria. The answer was so simple. But Lizzie thought it must be lonesome to be Tina, on an opposite schedule from everyone else's.

As if Tina had read her mind, she said, "On weekends, once I'm moved in and settled, I hope to spend time with my nieces and nephews. I have a lot of them in this town. That's why I moved here, to be closer to them." In her arms, Bella opened her eyes and looked in surprise at the new person.

Who are you?

Tina smiled down at her. "It's okay, little one," she murmured. And Bella closed her eyes, snuggled against Tina's chest, and went back to sleep. "Someday maybe I'll have kids of my own," said Tina, as if she were thinking out loud. "I have thought about adopting, but I'm not sure I'm ready to be a single mom. That's a big responsibility."

"My brother Adam is adopted," Lizzie said. "I can hardly remember the time before he came to live with us, though. It seems like the Bean has always been part of our family."

"The Bean?" Tina laughed. "Great nickname."

Lizzie told Tina how frightened she'd been about the responsibility of taking care of Bella. "I'm still scared, sometimes," she confessed. "Like when she won't stop crying."

"She must miss her mom and brothers so much," said Tina. "She must feel all alone in the world."

Lizzie smiled at Tina. She liked sitting on the steps with this new person, talking quietly as the rest of the neighborhood began to wake up. Tina was so easy to talk to. Maybe she would have a new friend next door, after all. But it was probably time to start getting ready for school. "I'd better go in," she said, standing up. "Want to meet the rest of my family?"

Tina shook her head. "Not when I'm in my p.j.'s," she said. "I'll stop over later and say hello." She handed Bella back to Lizzie, giving the puppy one last kiss on the head. "Nice to meet you,

Bella," she whispered. "Nice to meet you, Lizzie." Then she turned and headed back to her house.

Lizzie looked down at Bella, nestled in her arms. "Hey, little girl," she said softly. "You drank almost a whole bottle before we came out here. I bet you have to pee." She put the puppy down on the grass. Bella took a moment to wake up and get her legs under her, but then she began to totter off toward the apple tree. She sniffed the air excitedly as she picked her way through the grass.

Hello, world!

She went surprisingly fast on those little legs of hers. Lizzie loved the way her tail stuck straight up in the air.

Then Bella squatted and peed.

"Good girl!" Lizzie clapped her hands and cheered. "Your first time outside, just like a big girl. What a good, good puppy." She scooped Bella up and carried her back inside. Lizzie was surprised that nobody else was up yet, but when she checked the clock she saw that it was still early. In the kitchen, she put Bella into her box for a moment so she could get herself some cereal and warm some more formula.

Then, right there in her box, Bella squatted and peed again.

CHAPTER SEVEN

"Oh, Bella." Lizzie shook her head. "You just peed outside!" Lizzie knew Bella couldn't help it. That was just how puppies were, sometimes. When they had to go, they had to go. But now Bella's box was kind of gross. The newspaper lining was soggy, and after many, many pees and other messes the cardboard smelled stinky and was beginning to come apart. "I think it's time for a new box," Lizzie told the puppy.

She picked Bella up and tucked her carefully between two cushions on the couch, putting a pillow across the front so Bella could not climb out. "Hopefully you don't have any more pee in you," she said, as she petted the puppy's head. Bella gazed up at her with innocent eyes.

Pee? Me?

"I'll be right back," Lizzie told Bella. "I'm just going to run into the garage to find a new box."

The crying started before Lizzie was even out the door. Bella's whimpers were so heartbreaking. Every time she cried, Lizzie knew she was crying for her brothers and mother.

Lizzie dashed into the garage and rummaged around for the right-sized box, big enough so Bella would have one area for sleeping and one area for making her messes—but not so big that it wasn't cozy, too.

When she came back into the kitchen, the house was quiet. Bella was not crying anymore. Lizzie sighed with relief. Maybe Bella had fallen asleep on the couch, or maybe she was finally learning to be okay on her own. Either way, no crying was good news. Lizzie grabbed the chance to do what she had meant to do before: make herself a bowl of cereal and warm some formula. She bustled around the quiet kitchen as the sun's rays began to find their way in through the windows.

Then she stopped moving, to listen. Bella was *still* silent. Five minutes alone without crying. That was practically a record for her. Could something be wrong? Fear clutched at Lizzie's chest. She grabbed the bottle she'd warmed and ran into the living room.

"Oh, no!" She dashed to the couch. "Buddy, no! Bad boy." Buddy was curled up next to Bella on the couch, one paw over the tiny puppy's back as he licked her face.

Lizzie picked Buddy up and put him down on the floor. "You know you're supposed to stay away from her," she said sternly. Right away, Bella began to cry.

Lizzie sat down on the couch and took Bella in her arms. "It's okay, little one," she murmured. "The big doggy didn't mean to scare you." Bella's cries slowed as she settled into Lizzie's warm lap.

Buddy looked up at Lizzie, eyes wide and ears back, and lifted a paw.

I'm sorry. I didn't mean to be naughty.

Lizzie knew just what Buddy was trying to tell her. "I know you didn't mean to be bad," she said, reaching out to pat Buddy's head. Buddy scooted closer and leaned against Lizzie's knee, licking her hand as he gazed up at her. "You really are a sweetie," Lizzie told him. "You wouldn't hurt a fly."

Lizzie thought about that. Buddy really was a very gentle, sweet puppy. He had been so quiet and well-behaved around Bella, never jumpy or excited. She thought about what Tina Wu had said, that it would be hard for humans to make up for the warmth and comfort of another dog. Maybe it was wrong to keep Buddy separate from Bella. Maybe it was taking him *away* that had made the puppy cry. Maybe another dog's company was exactly what she needed.

Lizzie made up her mind. "Buddy, come on up," she said, patting the couch next to her. Why not try it right now, while she was there to watch them together? Eagerly, Buddy leapt onto the couch. "Can you be a nice, gentle boy?" she asked him, looking deep into his beautiful brown eyes. Buddy did not look away. His ears perked up and he thumped his tail.

Whatever you want, I can do it.

"Lie down, Buddy," Lizzie said. Obediently, Buddy curled up on the couch. Lizzie set Bella down next to him. Right away, Bella snuggled up to Buddy's belly. She sighed contentedly and scooched in even closer. Buddy gave her head a gentle lick and glanced up at Lizzie.

Is that okay?

"That's good, Buddy," said Lizzie. "Good boy." She petted him and her eyes filled with tears. So what if Buddy was a boy puppy? He could act just like a mother to Bella. Lizzie remembered pictures someone had emailed her once of a big brown dog who took care of a baby fawn. Animals could be foster parents just like people could.

Mom and Dad were surprised when they came downstairs and saw Buddy and Bella together,

56

but Lizzie quickly explained, telling them about how she'd met their new neighbor and how Tina had given her the idea to let Buddy cuddle with Bella.

"Dr. Gibson always gets in to her office early," said Mom, checking the clock. "I'll give her a call to ask if this is okay."

Dad sat next to Lizzie. "They look so happy together," he said. "Who knew Buddy could be a mom?"

A few minutes later, Mom came back into the room. "Dr. Gibson says it should be fine," she reported. "She said Ms. Dobbins was right—in most cases, a newborn pup should be kept separate from older dogs. But Buddy is such a sweetie, and he's very healthy, so there's no risk of disease. Dr. Gibson thinks it's a great idea. So do I. It'll sure make my day easier if I don't have to keep Buddy away, and Bella looks so much calmer, cuddled up with him." She came over and rested her hand on Lizzie's shoulder. "Good thinking, Lizzie."

Lizzie had just enough time before school to find and set up a new box for Bella, one that Buddy could fit into as well. And an hour later, she sat in class working happily on her brand-new, totally excellent idea for a Persuasive Essay.

CHAPTER EIGHT

Lizzie put down her pencil and shook out her hand. She smiled down at the paper on her desk. She was pleased with her new essay. And she'd finished it just in time: tomorrow was the day that everyone had to read their essays out loud in front of the whole class.

"What's it about?" Maria whispered from the desk next to hers. Maria was writing about "Horseback Riding: A Sport for Everyone." She had been inspired by a program at the stable where she took riding lessons. With the help of trained volunteers, disabled kids who could barely walk were learning how to ride horses.

"It's a surprise," said Lizzie, wiggling her eyebrows mysteriously. Even though she was pretty sure by now that Bella was going to make it, she still wasn't ready to tell Maria the secret. She wanted to wait until she was one hundred percent sure that Bella would live. She stretched and yawned. She was so, so tired from taking care of Bella. Fostering a newborn puppy had turned out to be way more work than she had expected. And it might still be weeks until Bella was old enough and strong enough to go to a new home.

Somehow, Lizzie managed to make it through the day without falling asleep at her desk. She brought her essay home from school so she could practice reading it out loud. Fortunately, Lizzie wasn't shy about standing up in front of the whole class to talk. She remembered last year when Brianna had started to cry during her oral report on the planet Neptune. That would never happen to Lizzie. But still, it was always good to practice in front of an audience.

When Lizzie pushed open the door at home, something felt different. What was it? Then she realized. No Buddy! For the first time she could remember, Buddy did not run to the door to greet her. No doggy kisses, no jumping up, no wagging tail. "Buddy!" Lizzie called. "Mom?" Where was everybody? Had something happened to Bella? Lizzie felt a twinge of fear.

"We're up here," called Mom, from her study.

Lizzie pounded up the stairs and down the hall. There was Mom at her desk. On the floor by her feet were Buddy and Bella, curled up cozily together in Bella's new box.

Mom grinned at Lizzie. "Hi, sweetie," she said. "Look at them. They're so happy together! Buddy hasn't left her side all day."

Buddy opened one eye and looked up at Lizzie. He thumped his tail.

See what a good job I'm doing?

His thumping tail woke Bella up. She stretched out a tiny pink paw and yawned a tiny pink yawn.

Is it time for more food?

Lizzie sat down next to the box to pet both puppies. "Good boy, Buddy," she said. "You're taking such good care of Bella." She stroked Bella's tummy with one finger. "Did she eat a lot today?" she asked Mom. "Her tummy looks very round."

Mom nodded. "She ate lots of the puppy chow slurry. I only had to give her one bottle."

"Yay, Bella!" Lizzie petted the puppy's soft fur. Carefully, she picked Bella up. She was definitely growing. Lizzie was sure the little girl puppy weighed more now than she had in the morning. Suddenly, just like that, Lizzie felt all her fear fall away. With Buddy's help, Bella really was going to make it. Buddy scrambled to his feet and put his head on Lizzie's knee so he could stay close to Bella.

Lizzie petted his head. "Mom, can I read you my Persuasive Essay?" Lizzie asked.

"Sure," Mom said. "I just finished some work, and I don't have to pick up the Bean from day care for another hour." Mom tapped a few keys on her computer and put it to sleep.

Lizzie put Bella back into her box, then rummaged in her backpack and pulled out her essay. She couldn't wait for Mom to hear it. But first, she had to get ready to read. She cleared her throat, stood up straight and tall just like Mrs. Abeson had taught them, and took a deep breath. "Okay. It's called—"

The front door slammed. "Where is everybody?" Charles yelled from downstairs. "How's Bella? Where's Buddy?"

Lizzie gave an exasperated sigh. Charles had

been riding his bike home from school lately with Sammy, his best friend from next door. They liked to take the long way home, exploring a different neighborhood every day, so he always got home later than Lizzie.

"We're all up here," Mom called. "Bella's fine. There are apples in the bowl on the counter."

Lizzie could hear Charles heading into the kitchen. She picked up her essay again. She cleared her throat, stood up straight and tall, took a deep breath, and got ready to read. "As I was saying, it's called—"

The doorbell rang.

Lizzie threw up her hands. Was she ever going to get to read her essay?

"Who could that be?" Mom said. She got up to go downstairs, and Lizzie followed her. There at the front door was Tina Wu.

"Hi," she said. "You must be Mrs. Peterson. Lizzie and I met this morning, but I wanted to introduce myself. I'm Tina Wu, your new neighbor. Thanks so much for the delicious lasagna."

"Come in, come in," said Lizzie's mom. "Lizzie told me about your topsy-turvy schedule, so I'll say good morning instead of good afternoon! You must be up early today."

Lizzie smiled, trying to hide her impatience. She was glad to see Tina again, but now she was going to have to wait to read her essay. She really, really wanted Mom to hear it.

Mom must have noticed. "Lizzie was just about to read an essay to me," she said to Tina. "Maybe she'd like a bigger audience."

"I'd love to hear it," said Tina.

Lizzie ran upstairs to get her essay. She decided to bring Bella downstairs, too. "Come on, Buddy," she said, nudging him out of the box. Bella whimpered a little, but stopped as soon as Lizzie picked her up. Buddy followed right at Lizzie's heels as she went back downstairs.

"Oh, can I hold her?" Tina asked, as soon as she saw Bella. "She's so adorable."

Lizzie brought Bella over, and Tina began to pet the tiny puppy. Bella looked completely at home cuddled up in Tina's lap. Buddy sat at Tina's feet, leaning against the couch and gazing up at Bella.

Lizzie picked up her essay and stood in front of the fireplace. She cleared her throat, stood up straight and tall, and took a deep breath. "My essay is called 'Anybody Can Be a Mom,'" she began.

CHAPTER NINE

Charles came in, still chewing on an apple. He joined Mom and Tina on the couch as Lizzie continued to read. "'This week, my family is fostering a newborn puppy named Bella. Bella's mom, Sissy, is sick, and Bella's brothers died. Bella could have died, too. But she is going to make it. And I learned something from watching our dog, Buddy, help take care of Bella.'" Lizzie paused to give her next words special weight. She made eye contact with each of her audience members. Then she went on.

"'It's this: If you give birth to a baby, then you become a mom. But there are other ways to become a mom, too. A person can adopt a baby. A chicken can sit on another chicken's egg. A dog can take care of a fawn. Or a puppy can take care of an even younger, newborn puppy.'" Lizzie looked at Bella on Tina's lap, with Buddy gazing up at her. That ache came into her throat again. But she managed to keep speaking.

"'Being a mom is about more than having a baby. Being a mom is about loving and caring for someone who would not survive without your love and care.'" Lizzie went on, trying to read with lots of expression and hand gestures, as Mrs. Abeson had taught them. Finally, she finished. "'In other words, if my puppy, Buddy, can be a mom, anybody can. Anybody can be a mom. All it takes is love.'" Lizzie looked up at Mom, Charles, and Tina. "The end," she added.

They all clapped and cheered. Lizzie saw Tina pull a tissue out of her pocket and blow her nose. "That was beautiful." She sniffled a little as she went back to stroking Bella.

Lizzie was impressed. Her speech had made somebody cry! "Thanks," said Lizzie.

"No, thank *you*," said Tina. "You helped me make a decision. I wasn't sure I was ready for this, but I think I am. Since I am up all night anyway, I would like to offer to take care of Bella for the night shift, so you all can get some sleep."

Mom turned to her. "Really? You would do that?"

"Sure," said Tina. "It's no trouble, really. She can sit on my lap while I work on the computer."

"What about Buddy?" Charles asked. He was on the floor now, with his arms around Buddy. "Won't he be upset if Bella goes away?"

Mom thought for a minute. "He usually goes to sleep for the night around the same time you two go to bed. As long as Bella isn't crying in the night, he probably won't wake up worrying about her." She turned to Tina. "If I bring her over to your house after Buddy's gone to sleep, it should be fine."

Lizzie nodded. She had to admit that she kind of liked the idea of not hearing Bella cry in the night. Maybe she could get some sleep before her big speech tomorrow. "I think that will work," she said.

Mom smiled at Tina. "It's almost dinnertime—for us, anyway. If you don't mind having lentil soup for breakfast, you're welcome to join us."

Tina looked surprised. Then she smiled. "That would be great," she said. "It would give Buddy and Bella a chance to get to know me a little more."

Bella sat on Tina's lap throughout dinner, and Buddy stationed himself right under her feet. Tina told the Petersons more about what it was like to work for a Chinese company, and they told her about some of the other puppies they had fostered. She especially liked the stories Lizzie and Charles told about the naughtiest puppies, like Pugsley and Rascal.

Later that night, just after Lizzie had gone to bed, she heard the back door close. She knew it must be Mom, bringing Bella over to Tina's. She held her breath, waiting to hear Buddy start whining when he realized "his" puppy was gone, but thankfully the house stayed quiet. Lizzie drifted off to sleep, practicing her Persuasive Essay speech even in her dreams.

She woke with a start early the next morning when Buddy stuck his cold, wet nose under her covers. Buddy whined a little and paced restlessly to the door of her room and back, as if he were looking for something. "She's not here, Buddy," Lizzie told him. She patted the bed. "Bella's safe and sound next door. Come on up and go back to sleep. It's barely light out yet." Buddy jumped onto the bed. "Mmm," said Lizzie. "Good boy." She pulled up her cozy covers and rolled over to go back to sleep. But then Buddy jumped off again and went back to the door, looking at her over his shoulder and whimpering softly.

"Okay, okay," said Lizzie. She stumbled out of bed and went to the window. Sure enough, there was a light on at Tina's, next door. Any minute, Tina would be coming outside to get her paper and watch the sun rise—and no doubt she would have Bella with her. Lizzie decided to take Buddy out to meet them.

Lizzie tiptoed downstairs and pulled on a jacket over her nightgown, then let herself and Buddy out the front door. Almost at the same time, Tina's door opened and she came out onto her front steps with Bella in her arms. Lizzie smiled and waved to Tina, and Tina waved back. Then Tina put Bella down on the grass.

When Buddy spotted the tiny puppy, he galloped over, screeching to a halt just in time to avoid knocking her over. He wagged his tail hard as he sniffed and sniffed. He put his front paws down and his rear end up in a "want-to-play?" pose, then sprang into the air and did three quick, joyful laps around Tina's front yard.

I'm so happy to see you!

Finally, he came back to Bella and settled down next to her so she could cuddle up close. With a contented little sigh, Bella snuggled up to Buddy's warm belly.

I'm happy to see you, too.

"How did she do last night?" Lizzie asked Tina.

"She was great," Tina answered. "She didn't cry at all—at least, as long as I was right there with her. She ate every few hours, but she slept a lot, too." Tina put a hand on Lizzie's shoulder. "Lizzie, what would you think if I said I'd like to adopt Bella? I've fallen completely in love with her and I'd like to give her a home here with me."

Lizzie's mouth fell open. "Really? That would be—that would be the best thing ever!" Lizzie had been worrying about how attached Buddy had become to Bella, and how hard it would be for him when they had to give her up to a forever family. But now Bella's forever family would be right next door.

Lizzie and Tina sat on Tina's front step as the sun rose, talking about how much fun it would be to watch Bella grow up, and how happy Buddy would be to have his beloved Bella as a neighbor.

But when Lizzie went inside to tell her family the great news, Mom just shook her head. "Lizzie," she said, "Bella may not be ours to give away."

CHAPTER TEN

Lizzie was stunned. "What do you mean?"

"I haven't had the chance to tell you yet," said Mom. "Ms. Dobbins called last night after you were asleep. Remember when she told us about Sissy, Bella's mother? She was so sick, but she's feeling a little better. Alexandra, her owner, is bringing Sissy up for a visit later this afternoon. You'll meet them both when you come home from school. Maybe Bella belongs with her mom now."

"But—" Lizzie couldn't believe it. "But Tina is the perfect person to adopt Bella. They belong together!"

"Technically, Bella still belongs to Alexandra," Mom said gently. "She's the one who gets to decide who Bella will live with. Maybe she wants to keep Bella herself."

Lizzie trudged off to school that morning, feeling miserable. This had never happened before. The Petersons had always been in charge of finding the perfect forever home for every puppy they fostered.

Mom had promised to explain the situation when Tina brought Bella over. Lizzie sighed. At least Buddy and Bella would not understand that they might soon be separated. And at least Lizzie would not have to be there to see Tina's sweet smile disappear when she heard the news.

Lizzie was not sure she would have the heart to give her Persuasive Essay speech in front of the whole class. She had been excited about revealing the secret of Bella to Maria, now that

Bella was not only thriving but had found a home. But now the home might not work out—and would Bella still thrive if she didn't have Buddy nearby?

When her turn came, Lizzie decided to pretend she was giving the speech to Alexandra, Ms. Dobbins's friend. If Bella's owner could hear the speech, maybe she would understand that Bella and Buddy should not be separated.

"Okay, Lizzie, you're on," said Mrs. Abeson, after Noah had finished his speech on "Why Kids Should Get to Choose Their Own Bedtimes."

Lizzie walked up to the front of the class-room, her heart beating hard. She turned to face the class and cleared her throat. She stood up straight and tall. She took a deep breath. And then she began, imagining that she was talking to Alexandra. "'Anybody can be a mom,'" she said, slowly and clearly.

A few minutes later, it was all over. Everyone

clapped, including Ms. Abeson. "Very good, Lizzie," she said. "Very convincing."

"That was great," Maria whispered, when Lizzie got back to her desk. "I can guess why you didn't tell me about Bella before. I'm glad she's going to make it."

Lizzie managed a smile. "Thanks," she said. "I was going to ask you home today to meet Bella. But now I don't know if you'll ever get to meet her." She told Maria about how Bella's real owner was coming to see her.

When Lizzie arrived home from school, she saw an unfamiliar red car in the driveway. Her heart began to thud again, just as it had before her speech. She could hardly stand the idea of saying good-bye to Bella, but she felt even sorrier for Buddy. The two puppies had become so close. How could anybody bear to separate them? She also felt terrible for Tina, who had given her heart to

Bella. It would be so hard to see her have to say good-bye. Lizzie squared her shoulders as she pushed open the front door, preparing herself for the bad news.

But it turned out that the news was not bad. It was not bad at all. There, in the living room, sat Tina with Bella in her lap and Buddy at her feet. She smiled and waved at Lizzie. So did Mom, and so did the woman who sat next to her on the couch. "Hi, I'm Alexandra," said the woman. She petted the pretty little red and white cocker spaniel who lay next to her. "And this is Sissy."

Lizzie smiled back. She had no idea why everybody looked so happy, but she had a pretty good idea that she would find out soon.

"Can I pet Sissy?" Lizzie asked. "She's pretty."

"As long as you're gentle," said Alexandra. "She's still not quite herself. That's why I'm so glad to hear that Tina would like to adopt Bella."

Lizzie felt her heart lift. "Really?"

"Isn't that great, Lizzie?" Mom asked, beaming.

"It's the right thing. I'm sure of it," said Alexandra. "I'm so grateful to your family for saving Bella's life." "And I can see that Bella and Buddy will be lifelong friends. Bella was so busy playing with Buddy that she barely sniffed at Sissy when we came in. That's good news, since Sissy would not be up to taking care of Bella the way Buddy and all of you have been."

"Lizzie even wrote a paper for school about Buddy being a great mom," said Mom. "It's a Persuasive Essay. She had to give it as a speech today."

"Mom!" Lizzie felt herself blush.

"Really?" Alexandra asked. "Would you give it again? I'd love to hear it."

"I'd like to hear it again, too," said Tina. "It was very persuasive. It convinced me to try taking care of Bella." She smiled down at the puppy. "And—I have some other news. Taking care of Bella convinced me that maybe I am ready to be a mom, after all. I've been thinking for a long time about adopting a baby girl from China, and I've finally decided to do it. I submitted the application just before I came over."

"Wow!" said Lizzie. "Really? Can I babysit?"

"Definitely," Tina said. "As soon as you're both old enough."

Lizzie stood there smiling. Everything had worked out so perfectly. Bella would grow up right next door, so she and Buddy could always be friends. And soon there would be a new baby next door, too!

"Speech, speech," called Mom. "Let's hear it."

Lizzie went to stand by the fireplace. She

cleared her throat. She stood up straight and tall, and took a deep breath. "This speech is dedicated to Bella and Tina," she said. "The newest members of our neighborhood." And then she began.

PUPPY TIPS

Newborn puppies grow and change so fast. If you ever get a chance to be around some new puppies, it might be fun to keep a journal each day and write down changes. You can record the day the puppies' eyes open, the day they learn to walk and explore their home, and the day they begin to get used to eating real food. Puppies are ready to leave their mom when they are seven or eight weeks old, and by then they are usually playful, mischievous, and a whole lot of fun.

Dear Reader,

My friends Chris and Kerry adopted a puppy, a tiny border collie mix, when she was only two weeks old and all alone in the world. They kept her warm and fed her from a bottle. Even though they weren't sure at first that she would make it, she did. Today Tassie is a strong, healthy dog who loves to run and play.

Yours from the Puppy Place,
Ellen Miles

P.S. If you want to read about another gentle puppy, check out SCOUT.

DON'T MISS THE
NEXT PUPPY PLACE
ADVENTURE!

Here's a peek at MOOSE!

Packing for his weekend away was easy. Getting up early? A breeze. The only hard part about going to Camp Bowser, thought Charles, was saying good-bye to Buddy. Now, sitting in the backseat of Aunt Amanda's van, Charles remembered how Buddy had looked up at him so hopefully when he put his duffel bag by the door. "Sorry, Buddy," Charles had told him, as he sat down to give him a hug. "You're not coming with me this time. I wish you could, but I think you might scare Moose. You stay home and keep Mom and Dad and the Bean company, okay?" Charles was not sure that Buddy understood, but he had given him lots of extra-special hugs and pats while he waited for Aunt Amanda to pick him up.

"Buddy's going to miss you and Lizzie this weekend," said Aunt Amanda now, catching Charles's eye in the rearview mirror. It was as if she had read his mind. "Your parents will, too. The house will be awfully quiet with both of you away."

Charles nodded. At the moment, he had a lump in his throat that made it hard to answer. He hoped he would not feel too homesick up at Camp Bowser. He looked over at Moose, who was snoozing in an enormous crate next to Charles's seat. A few other crates were crammed into the back of the Bowser Mobile, Aunt Amanda's van, holding more dogs that were on their way north for a weekend of fun in the country. Aunt Amanda had brought her golden retriever, Bowser, but she had left her three pugs home with Uncle James so the little dogs wouldn't scare Moose.

"We're going to have a good time, Moose," Charles said softly. "I bet you'll love it at Camp Bowser."

Moose opened his eyes and looked up at Charles, worried wrinkles furrowing his big forehead.

Really? Are you sure? Because I think it might be kind of scary.

Charles poked a finger through the crate to scratch Moose's ear. "It'll be fine. You'll see." Moose sighed and went back to sleep, head on crossed paws.

"I'm counting on you to keep a close eye on Moose this whole weekend and be his pal," said Aunt Amanda. "If there's another thunderstorm, or something else frightens him, the best thing to do is distract him so he doesn't focus on the scary thing. Talk gently to him, but don't baby him. Give him some treats so he has a happy experience instead of a frightening one. Can you do that?"

"Sure," said Charles. He patted his pocket, where there were four or five small dog biscuits. He always carried treats, just in case he met a stray dog or one he wanted to make friends with.

Then he reached into his backpack and pulled out the deck of cards he'd brought along. He had also packed *1-2-3 Magic*, the book he hoped to learn some tricks from. He planned to start with card tricks, since those seemed the simplest. There was only one problem. Even though *1-2-3 Magic* was supposedly for beginners, the author started the directions for every card trick with "Shuffle the cards . . ."

Charles did not know how to shuffle. When he and Sammy played War, which they sometimes did for hours at a time on rainy days, Sammy always shuffled. Charles suspected that Sammy sometimes shuffled some of the better cards into his half of the deck. It might be good if he learned to shuffle, too.

He opened the little box of cards and shook them out. "Oops!" They slid out of his hands and spilled all over the floor of the van.

"What do you have there, Charles?" Aunt Amanda looked at him in the mirror again.

"Just some cards." Charles scooped up as many as he could reach. He wasn't ready to tell anyone that he was learning magic. He wanted to surprise everyone once he had some great tricks ready. He split the deck into two parts and tried shoving them together, but most of them fell into his lap. He scooped them up again and tried another way, the way Sammy did it where he flipped the corners together. That was even worse. The ace of spades, the queen of hearts, and the four of diamonds ended up inside Moose's crate.

Charles kept picking up the cards and practicing. But by the time Aunt Amanda turned off the main highway and drove up a long, bumpy dirt road, he had still not learned to shuffle. When the van came to a stop, he shoved the cards into his backpack and zipped it shut. "Is this it?" he asked. "Is this Camp Bowser?"

"That's right," said Aunt Amanda. "Welcome."

ABOUT THE AUTHOR

Ellen Miles loves dogs, which is why she has a great time writing the Puppy Place books. And guess what? She loves cats, too! (In fact, her very first pet was a beautiful tortoiseshell cat named Jenny.) That's why she came up with a brand-new series called Kitty Corner. Ellen lives in Vermont and loves to be outdoors every day, walking, biking, skiing, or swimming, depending on the season. She also loves to read, cook, explore her beautiful state, play with dogs, and hang out with friends and family.

Visit Ellen at www.ellenmiles.net.

SOPHIE

Sophie knows she's special — now she just needs the perfect name to show it!

SOPHIE the AWESOME
by Lara Bergen
SCHOLASTIC

SOPHIE the HERO
by Lara Bergen
SCHOLASTIC

SOPHIE the CHATTERBOX
by Lara Bergen
SCHOLASTIC

SOPHIE the ZILLIONAIRE
by Lara Bergen
SCHOLASTIC